For Ewan, with love - AM
To Rosie and John - TA

First published in Great Britain in 2001 by Bloomsbury Publishing Plc
38 Soho Square, London W1D 3HB

Text copyright © Angela McAllister 2001
Illustrations copyright © Tim Archbold 2001
The moral right of the author and illustrator has been asserted.

A CIP catalogue record for this book is available from the British Library.
ISBN 0 7475 5580 X

Designed by Dawn Apperley

Printed in Belgium by Proost n.v.

3 5 7 9 10 8 6 4 2

P1-3

TH ⌐ OK

F
McA

Falkirk Council

Be Good, Gordon

Angela McAllister and Tim Archbold

BLOOMSBURY
CHILDREN'S
BOOKS

It was Tuesday night. Gordon's parents always went dancing on Tuesdays. His mother read him a story, then the doorbell rang.

'This is Lily Jigg-Popsicle, the new babysitter,' said his mother.
'Be good, Gordon.'

Gordon kissed his mother on her
deliciously perfumed ear.

He said goodnight to
Lily Jigg-Popsicle

and climbed into bed.

When the light was off Gordon climbed
out of bed ...

... led his dinosaurs into their cave ...

... put Bear's pyjamas on ...

... got back into bed, shut his eyes and went to sleep.

Gordon was always good on Tuesdays.

Suddenly something woke him up. 'Come on, Gordon. Don't go to sleep, let's play!' Lily Jigg-Popsicle was bouncing on his bed.

'I can't play now,' said Gordon. 'It's bedtime.'

'You don't have to go to sleep,' laughed Lily Jigg-Popsicle. 'Only tired people go to sleep.' And she rocked his bed like a shipwreck in a storm.

Gordon hadn't thought about whether he was tired or not. 'I must go to sleep,' he said. **'I have to be good.'**

Lily Jigg-Popsicle threw Gordon's bedspread into the air and it burst in a cloud of feathers. 'We could play snowstorms!' she giggled. 'And you could be the snow monster ...'

Gordon was quite interested in being the snow monster.
'But I have to be good,' he insisted.

'Well, Gordon,' groaned Lily Jigg-Popsicle, 'if you are going to be good then you can be the babysitter.'

And she lifted him right out of bed and bundled him downstairs. She put Gordon on the sofa and made him a cup of tea. She gave him some knitting, three socks to mend, two magazines and a plate of ginger biscuits.

'Night, night, Gordon,' she said, and ran upstairs.'

Gordon drank the tea,
ate the biscuits,
and mended the socks.
He didn't feel tired at all.

Suddenly Lily called out in a sing-song
voice. 'Gorrrrrrrdon, can I have a
drink of waaaater?'
Gordon fetched a glass of water.

Lily was sailing on
the high seas.

'Water, water
everywhere and not
a drop to drink!' she
cried. 'Thank you, matey.
Night, night.'

Gordon went downstairs again.
He sat on the sofa. He tried knitting,
but he could only do knotting.
    Lily called out again.
'Gorrrrrrdon, I've got a
tummy ache.'

Gordon fetched a hot-water bottle, like his mother always did. Lily was having a midnight feast.

'Food, glorious food!' she sang, and juggled with jam doughnuts.

Gordon gave her the hot-water bottle. 'I don't think your tummy ache can be very bad,' he said suspiciously.

Gordon read the magazines. He learnt how to cook pork chops and how to grow sunflowers.

Upstairs, Lily jumped so much that the ceiling shook and the lampshade dropped off.

Gordon opened his bedroom door.

Lily had made a Super-Springy-Lift-Off-Pad. 'Five, four, three, twoooo, One!'

She jumped, bounced and sprung up to the top of the wardrobe.

'Now I'm the man on the cheesy moon!' she laughed. **'Come on, Gordon!'**
Gordon thought hard. He wondered if springing was being good or bad?

'Come on,
Gordon!'
called Lily
even louder.

'I'll just
have one go,'
said Gordon.

So he bounced on the Super-Springy-Lift-Off-Pad. 'Five, four, three, twooo, One!' Gordon sprung into the air with a double somersault and landed on top of the wardrobe.

'Supersonic!' said Lily. 'You're a very good rocket, Gordon.'

An owl hooted in the garden. 'Now it's time for mud dancing,' announced Lily. They put on their wellies and went outside. Pond water and earth made the best sort of sticky mud.

'Whoop, whoop, whoop!' howled Lily, and they stamped around in mysterious circles. Gordon made a mud mask and galloped like the wind.

'Oooh! You're such a good galloper, Gordon,' said Lily. 'You can be Mudman chief.'

So they climbed into the tree house and sang Mudmen songs under the cheesy moon.

At last Gordon started to yawn.

'It must be bedtime,' he said. But Lily heard voices. She climbed up to the look-out.

'Look out!' she cried. 'They're coming home!'

The Mudmen galloped into the house, but forgot to take off their wellies. They covered the kitchen in mud.

'You do the mopping and I'll hide the doughnuts,' said Lily, and she bounded up the stairs. Gordon mopped the swampy kitchen.

'They're coming down the road,' called Lily. 'You fix the lamp-shade and I'll fix the bed,' and she tidied away the Super-Springy-Lift-Off-Pad.

Gordon balanced on the table to put back the lampshade.

'They're coming down the path,' shouted Lily. 'You jump into bed and I'll finish the knitting.'

So Gordon ran upstairs
and Lily ran downstairs.

Then they saw their
mud masks ...

'You're such a good friend, Gordon,' said Lily as they hurriedly scrubbed their soapy cheeks.

Just as the key turned in the lock Gordon tucked his damp smile under the blankets and shut his eyes.

On the sofa Lily Jigg-Popsicle sipped a cup of cold tea.

'We've had a lovely evening,' sighed Gordon's mother. 'Was Gordon good?'

'Oh yes!' said Lily Jigg-Popsicle. 'First he was good … and then he was very good … at everything!'

'I thought so,' smiled Gordon's mother, and she crept upstairs to kiss him goodnight.

'Night, night, Gordon,' she whispered. 'Thank you for always being good on Tuesdays.'

And the chief mudman grinned a cheesy grin, hugged his bear and nodded off to sleep.

Acclaim for *Be Good Gordon*

'Exuberant – and exuberantly illustrated … This is a book for children who want to grow up to be explorers and circus performers, rather than accountants, and for all the parents who will let them' *Guardian*

'A riotous tale of a topsy-turvy world … Great fun with crazy illustrations to match' *Junior*

'A story with a message, and a thrillingly subversive one at that: break the rules, have some fun!' *Independent*

'An amazing sequence of zany adventures' *Irish Times*

Enjoy more great picture books from Bloomsbury …

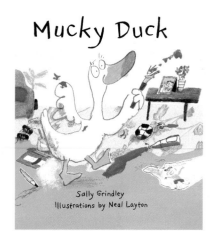

Mucky Duck
Sally Grindley & Neal Layton

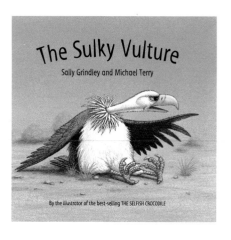

The Sulky Vulture
Sally Grindley & Michael Terry

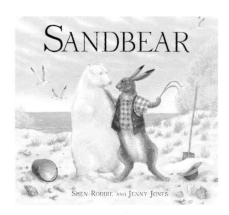

Sandbear
Shen Roddie & Jenny Jones

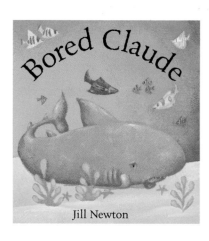

Bored Claude
Jill Newton